JONI'S WISH

BY JON PHILLIPS

ILLUSTRATED BY
CANDACE CAMLING

BookPress®

“Wake up, Joni! Today's the big day!” her dad shouted from the other room.

I can't wait to get my bicycle, Joni thought as she waved excitedly to Carl, who sat across the street from her room. *I'll finally be able to ride with the neighborhood kids!*

On their way to pick up her bike, Joni was thinking about taking rides around town. She felt very excited, but then thought about her neighbor. “Dad, can we take Carl with us on rides?”

“I'm sorry, Joni. Carl can’t ride a bicycle like you can,” her dad said. “He needs a different type of bicycle. One that he can pedal without using his legs.”

At the Bike Giveaway, Joni noticed many other children were around to get a bike too. When it was Joni's turn, she agreed to ride hers safely.

"It's important to always wear a helmet, use caution, and prioritize safety when riding a bicycle," the police officer said.

Back at home, Joni
rode her bike in the driveway
every day, and every day, she noticed
Carl watching her from his living room window.

I really wish he could ride bicycles
with me, she thought as she waved to Carl.

Then the doorbell rang, and she heard her dad say, “Joni, come here! You've got a visitor!”

“I heard you had a wish that your friend Carl could ride bicycles with you?” asked Stanley J. Heart. “What do you say we give him a bike as well?”

“Dad said Carl can’t ride a bike.”

“Don’t you worry,” said Stanley J. Heart. “I think we may have found a way.” Joni couldn’t stop smiling. She took Stanley’s hand, and together, they ran outside.

"I've never been on
a bike before!"
Carl shouted.
"This is going
to be so much fun!"

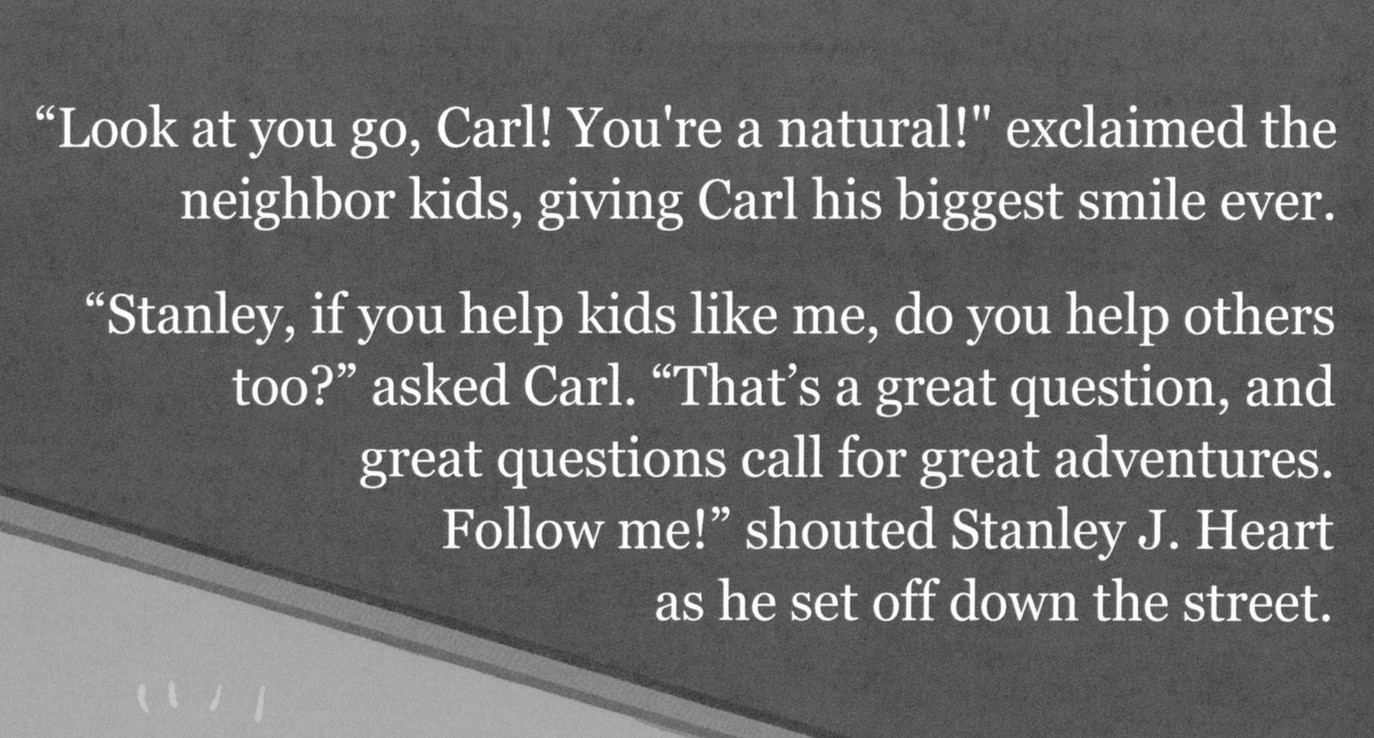

“Look at you go, Carl! You're a natural!" exclaimed the neighbor kids, giving Carl his biggest smile ever.

“Stanley, if you help kids like me, do you help others too?” asked Carl. “That’s a great question, and great questions call for great adventures. Follow me!” shouted Stanley J. Heart as he set off down the street.

Carl and Joni rode with the wind at their backs, and waved to a group of people. Carl was having a blast riding his bike for the first time.

"Look, Joni!
There's a kid just
like me!" shouted Carl
as he pointed at another child
in a wheelchair playing football.

Joni and Carl saw
many other kids
out having fun.
Carl had never imagined he could go on
adventures, but this bike ride was proving
to him that there were many things he could do.

Joni and Carl stopped to eat ice cream, and they saw a van drive by with kids inside. “We should race them!” shouted Carl, his bike giving him new confidence. “Let’s go!” Joni replied, knowing they would never be able to catch up.

Suddenly, Joni and Carl heard something in the distance that sounded like sirens. “What's that sound, Joni?” asked Carl. “I don't know. Let’s go see!” said Joni.

Joni and Carl rode to their next adventure. The sirens came from near the local hospital. Joni and Carl snuck up to the windows and saw nurses taking care of newborn babies.

"Joni, look at all the kids playing out here!" shouted Carl. "I have never been able to go to a playground and play like this before. I didn't know they had places where everyone was included."

"Race you to the slide!" shouted Joni.

variety
the children's charity

Joni and Carl had been riding all day, and they were coming to their last stop, a big building with a giant heart on its side.

"Should we go in?" Joni asked Carl. "I'm not sure. Do you know what's in there?" Carl asked.

"No, but let's go in anyway! It's just another adventure!" Joni said before Carl could stop her.

Joni and Carl had found their way into a Telethon where they saw lots of people answering telephone calls. Carl was given a microphone, and his latest adventure included asking people questions.

“Look, Joni!” exclaimed Carl. “I'm volunteering to help kids like me get bicycles too. This is so cool!”

Carl chose to interview Stanley J. Heart. “Thank you so much for my bike, Stanley J., I had so much fun on my many adventures today. I hope other kids like me get to experience this.”

"What did you and Carl do today?"
Joni's dad asked as he tucked her in.

"We did more than I can say!" Joni replied.
"I'm so glad Carl has a bike made just for him,
and he learned he can do anything he sets his
mind to. We had lots of fun!"

"Looks like you learned something too,"
Joni's dad said. "Get some rest, darling.
Sweet dreams."

variety
variety

Variety–the Children's Charity is dedicated to improving the lives of children who are at-risk, underprivileged, critically ill, or living with special needs.

Through their ***Kids on the Go!*** program, Variety helps children with special needs gain mobility, confidence, freedom, independence, and the chance to join in the life of their community by providing funding for specialized bicycles, gait trainers, standers, mobile standers, specialized strollers, specialized car seats, and more to families in need. What started as a program offering specialized bikes has expanded to fit the growing needs of children in our communities.

Alma Biermann

Charlie Curtis

For more information or to donate, visit **VarietyIowa.com**

ABOUT THE AUTHOR

Growing up, Jon Phillips would read anything he could get his hands on. He always envisioned himself writing his own book one day. As an analytical thinker, books were a place his imagination could run free. Jon sees parallels from his childhood which has driven him to where he is today. Jon works in the financial industry, remains active, and is involved with children's charities around the Des Moines, Iowa, metro.

Jon believes every child deserves a chance and it is because of this belief that he continues to find ways to be involved with philanthropic efforts. When the world changed due to a global pandemic, it was then that Jon decided to make his dream a reality and become an author. He hopes one day his book may inspire someone as he felt when he was a child.

Published by: Bookpress Publishing • P.O. Box 71532, Des Moines, IA 50325 • www.BookpressPublishing.com

Publisher's Cataloging-in-Publication Data

Names: Phillips, Jon, author. | Camling, Candace, illustrator.

Title: Joni's Wish / written by Jon Phillips; illustrated by Candace Camling.

Description: Des Moines, IA: Bookpress Publishing, 2022. | Summary: Joni finds out her neighbor Carl can't ride bikes with her, and it made her quite sad. Unbeknownst to Joni, someone heard about her wish, and it was granted!

Identifiers: LCCN: 2022913974 | ISBN: 978-1-947305-43-4

Subjects: LCSH Bicycles and bicycling--Juvenile fiction. | Friendship--Juvenile fiction. | People with disabilities--Juvenile fiction. | Sports for people with disabilities--Juvenile fiction.| BISAC JUVENILE FICTION / Disabilities & Special Needs | JUVENILE FICTION / Sports & Recreation / Cycling | JUVENILE FICTION / Social Themes / Friendship

Classification: LCC PZ7.1.P526 Jo 2022 | DDC [E]--dc23

First Edition

Printed in the United States of America

10 9 8 7 6 5 4 3 2 1